FRIDAY SURPRISE

Written by
Anne Fine

Illustrated by
Helen Flook

For Isaac and Olly.

A.F.

For Alex and Brenda.

H.F.

EGMONT

We bring stories to life

First published in Great Britain 2010
by Egmont UK Ltd
239 Kensington High Street, London W8 6SA
Text copyright © Anne Fine 2010
Illustrations copyright © Helen Flook 2010
The author and illustrator have asserted their moral rights.
ISBN 978 1 4052 49232
10 9 8 7 6 5 4 3 2 1
A CIP catalogue record for this title is available from the British Library.
Printed in Singapore.

Contents

Red Bananas

Yellow Armband

On Monday, Bryce had a swimming test.

'Swim all the way to the other side of the pool, please,' said Mr Reed.

Go for it!

Bryce sighed. 'But then I have to work my arms as hard as windmills. The water splashes in my eyes, and I hate that. And you already know that I can swim across the pool.'

'Yes,' Mr Reed agreed. 'But I still have to watch you do it one more time from start to finish before I can give you a yellow armband.'

People with yellow armbands could go anywhere they wanted in the pool. So Bryce had a go.

The water splashed horribly in his eyes and made him blink, over and over.

But he did make it to the other side.

'Good!' Mr Reed said. 'Now you've passed the test.'

He slipped the yellow armband on to Bryce's arm, and Bryce swam off.

'Ace!' he told himself. 'Now I can go anywhere I want in the pool, and when I get home, I can tell Mummy and Daddy!'

Wobble, wobble!

On Tuesday, Bryce asked Mummy if he could ride his bike all the way to the park. 'You know I'm steady enough,' he told her.

'I know,' said Mummy. 'But just to be certain, why don't we see if you can get as far as the shop on the corner without falling off?'

'Is it a test?' asked Bryce.

'Sort of,' said Mummy.

So off Bryce went on his bike, down the path
to the shop on the corner.

Wobble

The lumpiest place was outside the flower shop, where workmen had dug up the pavement twice in a row.

'Careful!' called Mummy.

The bike swayed from side to side. Bryce very nearly lost his balance. But in the end he managed to save himself, and made it past the last of the lumpy patches and on to the shop on the corner.

'Brilliant!' said Mummy. 'You did it! Off to the park we go!'

Hippopotamus and Elephant

On Wednesday, Mrs Miller called everyone on Blue table up to her desk as usual, one by one, so she could listen to them read.

Bryce handed Mrs Miller his reading book, but she pointed to a special sheet of paper on her desk. 'Today, can you read this for me instead?'

'Is it a test?' Bryce asked her.

'Only a little one,' said Mrs Miller.

'Oh, no!' Bryce muttered. 'That's my third test this week!'

But Mrs Miller was waiting, so he began to read the words out loud. It was a story about animals. He only had a problem with one or two of the longest words.

'First rate!' said Mrs Miller, when he had come to the end. 'You should be very pleased

with yourself. When you go home, you can tell Mummy and Daddy that I am sure that you are on exactly the right table.'

'Good!' Bryce said. 'And I can tell them that I can read "hippopotamus" now. And "elephant" too.'

Peeling Perfect Eggs

On Thursday, Daddy asked Bryce to help him peel the hard-boiled eggs for the salad supper. 'Take off the shell very carefully,' he told Bryce. 'We want to see nice smooth eggs, not eggs with lots and lots of tiny chunks picked out of them.'

'Is it an egg-peeling test?' Bryce asked him.

'Because I am fed up with tests. I've had one every day so far this week.'

'Surely not!' Daddy said. 'I can't believe it's only Thursday and you've had three tests already.'

'Yes, I have,' Bryce insisted. He counted them off on his fingers, one by one.

'On Monday, Mr Reed made me swim across the pool before I could have my yellow armband. On Tuesday, Mummy made me cycle as far as the shop on the corner before I could take my bike all the way to the park. On Wednesday, Mrs Miller gave me a reading test to check I should be on Blue table. And now it's Thursday, and you want me to peel perfect eggs.'

'Well,' Daddy said, 'if you've already had three tests this week, then we mustn't worry too much about the eggs. But not all tests are annoying. So maybe what you should do tomorrow is think of the sort of test that would be fun for you. The sort you would really, really enjoy.'

'Is that a whole other new test?' Bryce asked him. 'My fifth one in the week! The test for Friday?'

'I suppose it is, in a way,' said Daddy. 'A test to think of a test!'

And they both laughed.

Fun Test

Bryce thought about it as he went to bed.
How could he ever think of the sort of test
that would be fun? He knew that swimming

tests splashed his eyes. And maths tests could be quite hard. Reading tests often had long words he didn't know. Writing tests sometimes made his hand and fingers ache.

He thought about it when he woke on Friday morning.

How could he ever think of the sort of test he would really, really enjoy?

He thought about
it while he was
walking to school.

Then, suddenly, just as he walked in the
classroom, Bryce had a brilliant idea.

When they had finished in their workbooks and Mrs Miller said that everyone could draw a picture, Bryce put up his hand.

Yes, Bryce?

'Can I do writing instead?' he asked.

'Certainly you can,' said Mrs Miller. 'What are you going to write?'

'A test,' said Bryce. 'But not the usual kind. This is a test that will be fun for me and I'm really, really going to enjoy it.'

'That'll be interesting,' said Mrs Miller. And while the others were busy drawing their pictures, she came across to help Bryce with all the words that he didn't know how to spell.

At lunchtime, Bryce saw Mr Reed crossing the playground. Bryce hurried up and told him, 'I've written a special test for all the grown-ups who test me. And question number one is for you.'

'I'm ready,' Mr Reed said. 'Fire ahead.'

'What bit of swimming do I hate most?' Bryce asked him.

'Easy-peasy!' said Mr Reed. 'You hate the water splashing in your eyes. You're always going on about it, so I know.'

'That's right!' said Bryce. And he put a big tick and a smiley face next to the question for Mr Reed.

When he got back to the classroom, Bryce went up to Mrs Miller's desk. 'I didn't tell you,' he confessed to her, 'but one of the questions in the test you helped me write is actually for you.'

'Is that right?' Mrs Miller smiled. 'Since I'm the teacher, I certainly hope I can answer it.'

'It's easy-peasy,' Bryce said, and read out question number two. 'What were the two hardest words in my last reading test?'

'I seem to remember it was about animals,' said Mrs Miller. 'So was one of the words "crocodile"?'

Bryce shook his head. 'No.'

'Was it "kangaroo"?' guessed Mrs Miller.

'Wrong again,' said Bryce. 'But you sometimes give me three tries, so I am going to give you one more.'

' "Ant-eater"?' suggested Mrs Miller.

'No,' Bryce said. 'The hardest words were "hippopotamus" and "elephant".'

Mrs Miller looked crestfallen.

'Never mind,' Bryce said. 'I'm sure you'll do better next time. But I'm afraid that I can't give you a tick. Or a smiley face.'

'Fair enough,' Mrs Miller said. 'But you be warned. I shall try a whole lot harder to remember next time.'

At home after school, Bryce pulled the test out of his school bag and told his mother, 'I have a test question for you. It's question number three. What is the wobbliest bit of the bike ride to the shop on the corner?'

Easy-peasy!

'Easy-peasy!' said Mummy. 'That's the bit outside the flower shop where the pavement's lumpy and so you have to be really, really careful not to fall off.'

'Right,' Bryce said, and he gave Mummy a huge tick and a big smiley face.

Grumpy Face

As soon as Daddy had come back from the supermarket, Bryce spread the test out on the table and looked at question number four.

'I have a question for you,' he told Daddy, and read it out aloud. 'How many eggs did I peel perfectly last night when we had salad supper?'

Daddy scratched his head.

'I don't know. I can't remember. Was it four?'

'No.'

'Two?'

'No.'

'Three?'

'I'm afraid not,' Bryce told him sadly.

His father started to look anxious. 'Well, could the answer be one?'

'No!' Bryce said. 'And I'm afraid you're out of guesses now.'

'I failed that test, then,' Daddy said glumly. 'So tell me. How many eggs did you peel perfectly?'

'None,' Bryce said. 'In the end, you told me we mustn't worry too much about the eggs, and so I didn't and we ended up with little chunks picked out of every single one of them.'

'I didn't notice,' Daddy said.

'No,' Bryce agreed. 'That's because eggs taste the same, whether they have a few little chunks picked out of them by mistake, or not.'

He drew a large black cross next to question number four. And then, because he thought that Daddy really should have known the answer, he drew a very grumpy face.

Friday Surprise!

Bryce told Mummy and Daddy, 'There's one last question in my test.'

'Who is it for?' they asked together.

'Both of you,' Bryce said. 'And it's question number five. What do I want for my birthday?'

'That's not an easy one to answer,' said Mummy, 'because it changes every week.'

'Just last week, then,' said Bryce.

'A parachute,' said Mummy, except that I already told you that you can't have one.'

'A pretend beard,' suggested Daddy.

'A trip to Disney World,' guessed Mummy.

41

'One more guess each,' warned Bryce.

'A real submarine,' guessed Mummy.

'A real space ship,' guessed Daddy.

'Now you're being silly,' Bryce told them.

RATTLE

RATTLE

RATTLE

'I've told you both twice now that I want a
string puppet skeleton – one of those ones
where the bones really rattle.'

'So you did,' Daddy said. 'And I'd forgotten.'

'Twice,' Bryce couldn't help reminding him, and he put a very big cross and a not-at-all-smiley face next to the last question.

Bryce counted up.

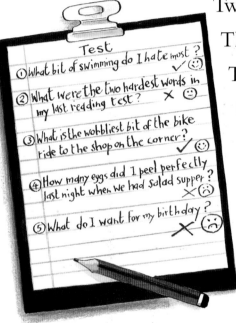

Two ticks.

Three crosses.

Two very smiley faces.

One medium face.

One very grumpy face.

One not-at-all-smiley face.

'So, go on. Tell us,' said Daddy.

'How did everyone do in your test?'

'Mr Reed did fine,' Bryce said. 'Mrs Miller didn't do too well, but she says she is going to try a whole lot harder next time. Mummy did all right. But, Daddy, I can't say that you did very well at all. In fact, you did terribly.' Bryce grinned. 'And out of all of us, I did the best.'

'How is that?' Mummy asked him. 'How can you possibly have done the best when you

didn't answer any of the questions?'

'Surprise!' said Bryce. 'Daddy told me that on Friday I should think of the sort of test I would enjoy. And I worked out that what I'd enjoy

most would be a test I gave to other people.'

'That is a surprise!' agreed Mummy, and she and Daddy laughed.

They watched as Bryce picked up a felt pen and drew a huge red tick and enormous smiley face for himself across the bottom of the test.

Then they went off to see who could make the very best pancakes. (It was another test.)